Mischief & Matchmaking: A "Pride & Prejudice" Variation

Mr. Darcy's Secret Stories

Abbey North

Published by Abbey North JAFF Books, 2022.

MISCHIEF & MATCHMAKING: A "PRIDE & PREJUDICE" VARIATION

First edition. July 20, 2022.

Copyright © 2022 Abbey North.

ISBN: 979-8201409869

Written by Abbey North.

Blurb

Matchmaking leads to mischief at Rosings Park.

WHILE LIZZY IS AT HUNSFORD to visit Charlotte, she becomes good friends with Anne de Bourgh. Anne reveals a shocking secret collection of tawdry romance novels, and the women soon form their own book society.

The merriment is interrupted by the arrival of Mr. Darcy and his cousin, Richard. Lizzy realizes Anne has a *tendre* for the dashing colonel, and Anne seems to think Lizzy is in love with Mr. Darcy. How perfectly preposterous. Mr. Darcy maintains his distrust of Jane's feelings and believes Lizzy is pursuing the colonel. He is determined to thwart that, of course.

Amid mischief and matchmaking from all sides, will there be a triple wedding in the future, or are Lizzy and Fitzwilliam too stubborn to admit their feelings and take steps toward a happy future?

While Abbey sometimes writes sweet JAFF, this is strictly SENSUAL.

Chapter One

WHAT A THIN, PALE, and cross creature Anne de Bourgh appeared to be. Lizzy felt unkind for the uncharitable thought, though an equally uncharitable one followed. She would make a proper bride for Fitzwilliam Darcy. He deserved that.

Despite the sting of her thoughts, she couldn't deny a completely different reaction than amusement or a sense of justice at the thought of Darcy leg-shackled to his cousin. It felt inexplicably like jealousy, and she quickly pushed back the response.

What a perfectly preposterous idea, to imagine she would be jealous of any woman deemed worthy of Fitzwilliam Darcy. She nearly laughed aloud at the idea, but she couldn't deny there was still an uncomfortable sensation in her stomach, and it was difficult to breathe for a moment as she imagined Miss de Bourgh walking down the aisle to meet Darcy to exchange vows. What a nauseating thought. Perhaps she should pity the young woman, and not simply because she looked ill. After all, she was to be settled as Darcy's bride. The poor thing.

Unfortunately, as they dined at Rosings Park, her dear friend Charlotte beside her, and Charlotte's husband and Lizzy's cousin, Mr. Collins, on the other side, Lizzy's impression of Anne didn't change. The girl was wan and ghostlike, barely saying a word or looking up from her plate. She was practically a nonperson, particularly when her mother dominated all aspects of conversation.

Lady Catherine de Bourgh overshadowed her daughter, whether inadvertently or deliberately. Either way, Anne was like a flicker from a candle and nothing more. By the time the meal had ended, Lizzy found herself firmly feeling sorry for the young lady, certain Mr. Darcy would be bored with her and likely setting up a mistress within a year of the marriage. That might be how some men of the *Ton* did things, but it left her feeling sympathetic toward Anne, though she still believed Darcy deserved a miserable marriage.

LIZZY WAS OUT WALKING the next morning, admiring the sprawling beauty of Rosings Park. Lizzy had felt free to wander around each morning of her visit. She'd been here two weeks so far, and it still seemed like she discovered something new with every walk.

This morning, the surprise discovery ended up being Miss Anne de Bourgh herself, who was currently sitting on a low stone wall that looked like parts of it had broken off over the years. It had likely been part of an old fence or house, but it was impossible to tell these days.

She was concerned for Anne, thinking the woman might have gotten ill, especially since they were a good two miles from Rosings Park's main house. She hurried forward, tucking her parasol under her arm. She'd brought it on the off chance the gray tinging the sky would yield rain, but so far, it had been a lovely morning. She hadn't even used it to prevent freckles. "Miss de Bourgh, are you ill?"

Anne looked up then, and Lizzy realized she been crouched forward in such an angle because she was reading something on her lap, not because she was holding her stomach or visibly in pain. Intrigued, Lizzy grew closer, slightly amused by Anne's alarm. She seemed to be hastily hiding whatever the book was between her skirts, and Lizzy couldn't stifle a surge of curiosity.

When the book slipped from the dress and landed on the ground, she knelt to pick it up, looking at the lurid cover. It promised to be a dashing adventure story featuring a charming pirate rogue. Lizzy's eyes widened as she looked at Miss Anne, surprised to see Darcy's cousin's choice of reading material. "What is this?"

"It is nothing," said Anne hastily as she reached for the book.

Lizzy took a step back, wanting an extra moment to peruse it. She opened the cover and started to flip through it, gasping when she saw a couple of words with which she wasn't familiar. *Cunny* and *quim* jumped out at her, and her eyes widened as she read the context, quickly figuring out exactly to what the author referred. With a shocked wheeze, she closed the book and handed it back to Anne. "Oh, my."

Anne was flushing spectacularly now as she shifted slightly on the stone wall, not looking at Lizzy. "I would appreciate your discretion, Miss Bennet. If my mother were to find out about these..."

She sat down beside Anne on the stone structure. "You have more?"

Anne blinked, and she slowly nodded. "I have a hidden collection." She seemed to feel daring when she admitted that, as though she was somewhere between nauseated and amused. She could vomit or giggle at any moment, it seemed.

Lizzy was reluctantly fascinated as well. "I assure you of my discretion, but might I impose upon you for some reading material? I confess, I have never read anything like that, and I am morbidly curious."

Anne was still flushing, but she nodded and got to her feet, indicating Lizzy should follow her. She led her to an old cottage a couple hundred meters from the stone structure, looking around furtively before shoving aside a heavy metal frame that could have been from a bed, or perhaps a carriage. It was difficult to tell with parts of it missing, but it was obviously heavy, making the young woman grunt at the task.

She gestured for Lizzy to follow her inside, and in seconds, she was lighting a lantern. Apparently, she had a lot of practice with the striking kit, and the lantern provided enough illumination to see the cottage wasn't as bad on the inside as it was on the outside.

"What is this place?"

"It is my secret hideaway, Miss Bennet." Anne looked fretful for a moment. "Perhaps I should not be showing you this, but I implore you to understand my mother allows very little freedom. Many times during my childhood, I was forced to sneak out to be able to enjoy some fresh air and sunshine. During one of my wanderings around the property, I came across this cottage. I have spent some time fixing it up as much as possible on the inside, but as you can see, the light is hardly conducive for reading."

Lizzy nodded her agreement. Strong morning sunshine, other than tinged with the gray in the sky, should filter through, but the windows were too dirty, and everything was slightly gloomy. However, she could see touches where Anne had made improvements, including on the bed. There appeared to be a fresh blanket, and she went there now.

Instead of getting onto the bed though, Anne knelt on the floor, using what looked like a discarded chair leg placed carelessly on the floor to raise a section of floorboards. They lifted with hardly a creak, indicating they were well used to the torsion. She moved aside the panel that had been glued together to reveal a hollowed-out niche in the floor.

Fascinated, Lizzy moved closer, holding her breath slightly when Anne pulled out a long, narrow chest. She sat on the floor and opened it, looking apprehensively at Lizzy as she gestured to the contents.

Lizzy looked down, realizing the small chest was stuffed full of books. She reached for one randomly, flipping through it and blushing when she reached the part of the stablemaster teaching the young mistress of the house how to ride properly, but there wasn't a horse mentioned on the page. She flushed and flipped open the lace fan with a practiced motion to wave near her face. "My goodness."

"You are welcome to borrow them as you wish, but I do ask that you return them and hide them each time. I cannot imagine a scenario where my mother would search all the abandoned buildings on Rosings Park, but if it were accidentally discovered, and if she ever realized they belong to me..." She paled even further, making her look like a phantasm. "It would be disastrous. It would be even worse if she believed they belong to a staff member and discharged someone, causing them to lose their livelihood because of my shameful hobby."

Lizzy cleared her throat. "You have my word that I will be the soul of discretion. I am not entirely sure I will be able to read these, because they seem quite scandalous, but I shall make every effort." With a grin, she slipped the book into her reticule. "I shall return it as I found it. You have my word."

Anne seemed satisfied by that. "I thank you, Miss Bennet. I fear there is something wrong with me to enjoy this type of reading material. Yet when I read them, I cannot help but devour them and wish I had a man such as the ones between these pages."

"I do hope you will not be disappointed with Mr. Fitzwilliam Darcy when you are married, because I cannot imagine him being a man to rise to such occasions." Lizzy tried to stifle a giggle at the image of Fitzwilliam Darcy teaching any woman to ride without a horse.

The flight of fancy took a disconcerting turn when in her imagination, the woman mounting Darcy like a horse was herself. She shook her head, casting off the idea with what she told herself was disgust. Who would want to sit on Darcy's back while he walked around on his hands and knees anyway? The idea of putting a saddle on him made her want to giggle though.

Anne looked appalled. "Oh, I do not plan to marry Fitzwilliam. I could never love him the way I do..." She trailed off, biting her lip.

Lizzy arched a brow. "You do not love Mr. Darcy?"

Anne frantically shook her head. "Not a whit, except in a sisterly fashion. Mama does not care for my opinion on that, and indeed, she has no regard for Fitzwilliam's input either. She is determined we will marry, and in her mind, that is the end of it." With a surprising amount of strength, Anne firmed her shoulders and sounded resolved when she said, "It is not the end of it for me though."

"There is another?"

Anne hesitated before slowly nodding. "I have tried not to love him, but I fear it is too late. Of course, he shall never notice me. He must seek out an heiress to maintain a decent living, with being the second son of an Earl, since he has long held that he does not wish to remain in the militia for years to come. I am an heiress, but I do not believe he has ever regarded me in such a way."

Lizzy hesitated, uncertain how to reply. She could see where a man might miss Anne's appreciation for him, since she was so plain and quiet. As she looked closer, she realized Anne wasn't terribly plain. Truthfully, she had beautiful bone structure, and if her skin weren't so pale, she'd probably look quite lovely. It was difficult to tell about her hair with it covered by a bonnet, but it could be arranged to enhance her features. "Does this man have any idea how you feel?"

"As I said, I doubt he has even regarded me that way."

"I take it you have known him a long time?"

Anne hesitated. "All my life."

"And he regards you as a friend?"

"Or perhaps even a sister." She was obviously miserable as she said that. "He is my cousin, but..." She trailed off and then looked horrified. "Oh, I did not mean to say that."

Lizzy didn't know the intricacies of the Fitzwilliam and the Darcy family trees, but it wasn't Darcy by Anne's own admission. "You may tell me with full assurance that I will not divulge your secret, even to my sister Jane—though she is in London, so I suppose that hardly counts for vouching at this moment. If you wish to discuss it, I am open to hearing about it." Lizzy wanted to be helpful but also couldn't deny she was dreadfully curious. It was a terrible trait but was a personal failing with which she lived.

After the longest hesitation, leading Lizzy to believe Anne wouldn't say anything further, the other woman whispered, "Colonel Fitzwilliam."

"I do not believe I know him. Is he at Rosings Park?"

She shook her head. "He is currently with the militia, but he should be visiting again soon. He comes at least twice a year, and I do believe you will like Richard if and when you get to meet him, Miss Bennet." Her lips turned down slightly. "Of course, I hope you shall not like him too much, or that he will not like you too much."

Lizzy smiled. "I am certain you are safe in that regard, and even if he fell madly in love with me, which seems unlikely, you mentioned he requires an heiress. I am nowhere near being an heiress, I can assure you."

Anne looked relieved. "Thank you for your assurances, Miss Bennet. I do look forward to getting to know you better."

"Of course. We must have our own book society." She had a splendid idea then. "Would you find it shocking if I shared this book with Charlotte, should she have interest?"

Anne's mouth gaped open. "Mrs. Collins? I can hardly credit the idea of her wanting to see such a thing."

Lizzy chuckled in a knowing way. "Believe me, Mrs. Charlotte Collins has not always been so prim and proper. She and I grew up together, and though she was older, we were quite close. I do not believe she would be as shocked as you might imagine, but I will refrain from showing it to her if you wish?"

"I suppose I do not mind, but perhaps you could leave my name out of it, at least until you are certain she is interested in these foolish romantic books?"

Lizzy nodded her agreement, looking at the box once more before Anne closed it and stowed it under the floorboards and put the cleverly designed piece of wooden panel back into the hole it fit in. "Tell me, where do you get your collection?"

Anne's flush deepened. "When I was slightly younger, before Mrs. Jenkinson was my companion, I had a younger companion. When we were in London, I discovered her secret trove of these books, so she showed me a bookstore where I might acquire them. I dare not order them directly to the house, lest they be intercepted, but when Mama takes me to London twice a year, I must always visit the shop and acquire what they have. That is why my collection is so scant after six years of accumulating."

Lizzy felt a pang of sadness for her friend, for if she'd been acquiring books for six years, her collection was indeed meager. There couldn't be more than twenty-five books. "I confess to being curious, and if I enjoy this reading material, perhaps you would be so kind as to pass along the bookshop's name?"

Anne hesitated for a moment and then shrugged. "I suppose that could be arranged, but it must be a carefully guarded secret. There are certain things available in the establishment that would bring great trouble to the owners if it were discovered."

Lizzy nodded, understanding the need for discretion. The two of them soon departed from the cottage after sliding the metal piece back in front of the door. From a distance, it didn't like it had been disturbed at all, though up close, there were gouges in the wood where the metal had been moved back and forth until it formed a familiar groove. "I must confess, I never would have imagined you having something quite so interesting as all this, Miss Anne."

Anne smiled. "I do seem rather like milquetoast, do I not?"

Lizzy hesitated, afraid she had said too much that would be construed as an insult.

"It is true though. It is almost impossible to exert personality around my mother, and that I have retained any at all over these years being raised under her is probably quite miraculous." She grinned in spite of her dour words. "I suppose I must have a strong-willed personality. I can recall a few whippings in my earlier days before I learned to pretend to submit."

Lizzy liked how she phrased that, and she grinned. "If it would be convenient, why don't you come to Hunsford for tea tomorrow afternoon, and perhaps we can discuss reading material then?"

Anne nodded her agreement, and they started walking back to Rosings Park. As they parted near the walkway that would lead Anne home and Lizzy on to Hunsford, she asked, "Have you considered telling the man about your *tendre*?"

"I could never be so bold as to reveal that, particularly since I fear he sees me as nothing more than a sister. It would fundamentally change things between us." That clearly upset her.

Lizzy nodded her understanding, and she didn't push her friend to try a different method. In many ways, Anne reminded her of Jane, who was reserved and not one to show her feelings openly.

With a word of parting, she returned to the rectory. Fortunately, Mr. Collins was out, and Lottie must have accompanied him. That allowed Lizzy ample time to settle into her room and start reading the book Anne had loaned her. She dared not read it in the parlor, lest someone discover her immersed in such tawdry words.

Lizzy was surprised to find herself quite taken with the story of a rebellious young lady refusing to marry the man her father had chosen for her because she had fallen in love with a stablemaster. The more she read, the hotter it got, until she popped open a couple of buttons at her neckline and continued to fan herself as she read.

When she reread the scene of riding lessons, she soon realized she'd had it all backward in her mind. It wasn't a matter of a woman sitting on a man's back like one would ride a horse. No, it was far more intriguing, and this time when she pictured Mr. Darcy being ridden, once again with her face firmly on the image of the woman astride him, she was more aroused than dismayed by the idea. "Oh, my," she said aloud as she continued to fan herself.

Chapter Two

"LIZZY," SAID CHARLOTTE in a whisper, trying to get her attention.

Lizzy increased her pace to catch up to Charlotte, who had feigned needing to re-button her shoe as an excuse to break away from Mr. Collins as the three of them walked toward Rosings Park. Sir Lucas and Maria had departed a few days ago. "Here is that book."

Lizzy took it quickly, slipping it into her reticule beside the one she had recently borrowed from Anne as well. Over the last two weeks, she and Charlotte had been busily working their way through Anne's meager collection, and she was sad to note they were both almost to the end.

The books weren't very long, and they were somewhat melodramatic and full of ridiculous ideas, but they were terribly romantic, and they were spicier than anything Lizzy's imagination had been able to conjure before reading them. As she had expected, Charlotte had been receptive to the idea once Lizzy had finished reading "The Stablemaster's Bride" and offered it to her friend discreetly during tea.

Charlotte had not been quite as shocked at the contents as Lizzy, for she was a married woman, but she confessed to Lizzy later that there were many things in that book she didn't realize were possible. Lizzy hadn't inquired if she planned to try them with Mr. Collins, because that was an image she didn't want in her mind.

"I cannot believe how fast we read these." She whispered that to Charlotte as they continued to walk a few feet behind Mr. Collins on the way to Rosings Park. "Anne just brought them yesterday afternoon."

Charlotte let out a small giggle. "I fear I cannot stop myself. 'The Pirate's Wench' drew me in."

Lizzy nodded her agreement. She had read that book yesterday while Charlotte read "The Highwayman's Captive," and they had traded just this morning. Unfortunately, they were running low on books, and Lizzy hoped to procure more for them if she could find a way to visit the London bookshop when she went to join Jane and the Gardiners at Gracechurch Street in a few weeks.

"You two are quite slow this evening," said Mr. Collins with a hint of rebuke. "It would not do to be late to see Lady Catherine. I daresay, it would be the height of poor manners."

"I am sorry, husband," said Charlotte in a soothing tone. "There was a pebble in my shoe."

Mr. Collins nodded briskly, waiting for them to draw near. Lizzy and Charlotte exchanged a glance, but Lizzy did her best not to giggle. Charlotte seemed to be tamping down the urge as well, and by the time they presented themselves at Rosing Park, they were every inch the respectable young women they seemed to be. No one would guess there was scandalous reading material in Lizzy's reticule that she planned to return to an equally proper Miss de Bourgh that evening.

Unfortunately, there was a snag in Lizzy's plan. As soon as they entered Rosings Park, she barely held back a grimace at the sight of Mr. Darcy. Beside him stood a handsome man in the militia uniform, and since he was roughly the same age as Fitzwilliam Darcy and Anne de Bourgh, she concluded he must be Richard Fitzwilliam, whom she'd heard about at Netherfield.

It made sense he might be the object of Anne's affection, so she slanted a glance her way. She looked positively miserable, which confirmed that supposition even before being properly introduced to him.

When she turned to face Fitzwilliam, he took her hand and kissed it lightly on the back of her glove, but it seemed to be uncomfortable for both of them. He quickly dropped it, and she took a step back. "I did not expect to see you here, Mr. Darcy."

"Indeed, why would you not? After all, Lady Catherine is my aunt. As far as I know, she is nothing to you."

"She is Mr. Collins' very dear patroness, and she condescends to entertain us a few times each week." Lizzy couldn't help infusing the words with a hint of mocking, but she was surprised when Darcy seemed like he might smile.

Of course, he quickly restrained the urge and returned to looking stern and unapproachable. "I see. I did not realize you would be visiting Mrs. Collins at this particular time."

"Had you, I am confident you would have arranged to reschedule your visit. Am I correct in that thinking, Mr. Darcy?"

"It would be rude of me to consider answering that question, for to call a guest incorrect would be the height of ill conduct."

She frowned, not entirely certain what his answer meant. Would he have rescheduled or not? Sometimes, she wished society allowed for more open conversation.

"You must be here for your semiannual visit. Anne... Miss de Bourgh mentioned that to me recently." As she spoke Anne's name, she turned to look at her friend, who was talking to the Colonel. Her eyes widened slightly when Colonel Fitzwilliam took a step closer, bending to whisper something in Anne's ear.

It made the woman giggle and judging by their stances—though Lizzy was no true expert on passion in body language—she wasn't entirely convinced Anne was correct in her assumption the colonel had never noticed her in any way that wasn't sisterly. In fact, he seemed to be noticing her quite well, but Anne quickly withdrew, and the colonel stepped back. If she wasn't wrong, he let out a sigh, perhaps of weariness. The moment had passed, and he soon turned to Lady Catherine.

When she looked back at Darcy after he cleared his throat, she realized he was scowling at her. "What has brought such a look of censure to your face, Mr. Darcy? I have no doubt it is directed toward me."

His brows joined together heavily. "If you are speculating my cousin will make a fine victim to take home to offer up to your mother as a matrimonial sacrifice, I must warn you now that he is only able to—"

"Marry an heiress," said Lizzy with a breezy tone. Seeing his eyes widen with surprise, she smiled. "Miss Anne also mentioned that."

"I take it you have become friendly with my cousin?"

"I thought she was your betrothed," said Lizzy, barely biting back the urge to laugh again.

He scowled at her. "Some things are not up for discussion, Miss Bennet."

"Do not worry, Mr. Darcy, for I do not wish you to take me into your confidence. Besides, I already know Anne..." She trailed off and started to walk away. She wasn't entirely surprised when Darcy followed her a moment later as she made her way to the pianoforte.

"Anne what?"

She bit her lip as she looked over her shoulder. "Anne has informed me she has no wish to marry you." She had expected his ego to slightly deflate, so his impassive reaction was rather disappointing.

He shrugged slightly. "She and I are in agreement on that fact and have been for many years. If only my aunt would listen to us." He shrugged again. "It matters not, for neither Anne nor I have found anyone whom we wish to marry, so we allow Lady Catherine her delusions for the time being."

"That is remarkably kind of you, but I fear if you allow Lady Catherine her delusions, you might end up regretting it when she inevitably takes issue with you and Anne ignoring her edict. Presumably, with you being a man of great income and single, you must surely be in want of a wife, so you might be courting her objection by allowing her beliefs to remain intact."

His lips clamped. "I shall take a wife if and when I am prepared to do so and not a moment sooner, Miss Bennet." He gave her a scathing look. "My aunt's opinion will hold no sway on that." He eyed her through squinted lids. "You are certainly not suggesting I should search for a bride now? Have you a candidate in mind?" His tone revealed his lack of interest in her input.

She quickly lifted a gloved hand. "Calm yourself, Mr. Darcy, for I was not suggesting myself for the role. Indeed, I cannot imagine a worse fate. I had known you but a month before I decided I could never marry a man like you."

"I do not recall asking you to do so." He glared at her. "You should be honored to marry a man like me."

Lizzy couldn't help rolling her eyes. "I do acknowledge you are much above me in station and status, not to mention wealth, but we would have a fearfully boring match, do you not agree, Mr. Darcy?"

He snorted slightly. "I do believe it would be ill-advised, but I do not believe it would be boring, Miss Bennet." With those unsatisfying words, leaving her to doubt everything that had occurred, he nodded to her and moved across the room to speak with Miss Anne.

Lizzy was still trying to sort it out as they moved to the dining room for dinner, perplexed by Darcy's responses. There had been almost an edge of flirtation to his words, but hadn't there been in hers as well? She hadn't truly been exerting feminine wiles on her loathed enemy, had she?

As she mentally reviewed the conversation, she couldn't help recalling instances where it might seem as though she were fishing for a compliment or wanted some type of assurance from him. Thankfully, he hadn't offered it, and she dismissed the whole idea as she took a seat at the table.

Fortuitously, she found herself seated across from Anne and beside the colonel, so she spent the next several minutes engaging him in conversation. When she learned the colonel liked to walk during early mornings, she said, "As do I. Perhaps we shall see each other in the morning, Colonel Fitzwilliam."

"Perhaps, Miss Bennet." He looked at Anne. "Do you still walk in the mornings?"

Before Anne could answer, Lady Catherine spoke up. "Do not be ridiculous, Richard. Anne's constitution does not allow for such things. She must remain in her room and rest for a good part of each day to have strength to dine with me. I will acknowledge her weaknesses, but I shall not allow her to avoid her duty of having dinner with her own mother."

If Richard took issue with Lady Catherine's words, it didn't show, though perhaps his lips twitched a little. "Of course, we would not want to inconvenience you by tiring out Anne before dinnertime, Aunt Catherine, for it takes great fortitude to dine with you."

The lady in question frowned at him, clearly disliking him using that honorific instead of Lady—or perhaps catching his subtle joke at her expense. Lizzy had to swallow her smile, hiding it in her glass of wine as she took a sip, realizing she was going to like the colonel quite well.

Only when she looked up and met Fitzwilliam Darcy's disapproving gaze did she realize he must have reached the same realization. Clearly, he had cast a different perception on her interest, and he was incorrectly assuming she had the beginnings of a *tendre* for Colonel Fitzwilliam. Darcy was a foolish man, but she wasn't about to make it easy on him by assuring him he was wrong in that matter, as well as most others.

SHE FOUND HERSELF WALKING beside the colonel the next morning, and it soon became a morning habit for each of them to meet and walk together. On the fourth morning of strolling together, Lizzy felt brave enough to broach a more personal topic with him. "You seem quite fond of Miss Anne."

The colonel hesitated and nodded. "Yes, I am quite fond of Anne. She and I exchange letters many times per year. We grew up together."

"She must be like a sister to you."

He stumbled, almost missing a step with how quickly he looked away. He seemed flustered, and Lizzy hid a smile at his reaction. "We did grow up together, but I do not regard Miss Anne as my sister."

"I do not believe she regards you as a brother either, Colonel Fitzwilliam." It was as close as Lizzy dared come to revealing Anne's secret affection, for she had no wish to betray her friend.

The colonel's eyes widened, but he didn't ask for clarification or confirmation. He just cleared his throat and said, "I fear I must find a bride soon, so perhaps I will ask for her input. She must know a lovely and willing heiress."

Lizzy grinned. "Of course you must, for she is a lovely heiress, is she not? It makes sense that she would move in the same circles as other lovely heiresses." She hoped she'd given him something to think about as they resumed walking at a more rapid pace. "You should come for tea this afternoon, Colonel, and do bring Miss Anne. I haven't seen her for a few days, since you and Mr. Darcy arrived."

The colonel hesitated and then nodded. "Am I correctly sensing there is some friction between you and Mr. Darcy, Miss Bennet?"

"You are most astute." Either that, or she and Darcy were both terrible at hiding the animosity between them. It could be that.

"You have barely known each other, is that right?"

Lizzy shook her head. "I have met him before." As quickly as possible, she gave a brief overview of having met him at the Assembly ball.

He was soon howling with laughter as she described what a mess he had made for himself with his imprudent words. "That does sound very much like Fitzwilliam." There was a strong hint of affection in his tone. "He is not one for social engagement, and I fear it is awkward for him. The skill does not come easily to Fitzwilliam as it does to some."

"I shall concede he lacks your easy manner, charm, and wit, Colonel Fitzwilliam. He certainly made a memorable impression upon me and the Meryton Assembly ball though."

"Indeed. Perhaps he has made another type of impression on you as well?"

Lizzy frowned at him probing her feelings about Mr. Fitzwilliam Darcy as she had tried to do with him and Anne. Had he picked up on her not-so-subtle interrogatives and decided to reciprocate, or was it simple conversation? Or had he imagined there was something there that was not?

Either way, she was glad to move past the subject with a quick change of topic, and they were soon discussing the numerous roses Lewis de Bourgh had planted for Lady Catherine throughout their marriage. It appeared he had been lovingly devoted to his wife, and though Lizzy could hardly imagine what the dead man had seen in Catherine de Bourgh, she still found it rather romantic to imagine him making such extravagant gestures on a regular basis. She could only hope Lady Catherine had appreciated them and Mr. de Bourgh.

Chapter Three

UNFORTUNATELY, WHEN Richard and Anne turned up for tea, they brought along an unwanted guest. Fitzwilliam Darcy trailed behind them, and he seemed to realize he had not been included in the invitation, because he was slightly ill-at-ease. Or perhaps it was the lack of social graces his cousin had alluded to that made him visibly uncomfortable. She doubted it though. Lizzy was certain Darcy didn't want to be there any more than she wanted him there.

In spite of that, she decided to have some sport, so she sat beside him on the settee as Mrs. Tesch poured tea for all. Mr. Collins was out visiting a parishioner, so they didn't have to deal with his overbearing and obsequious presence, to Lizzy's relief. Charlotte appeared relieved as well, and she was more relaxed as they took tea.

On the surface, the conversation was completely respectable, but when Anne made mention of riding lessons, Lizzy and Charlotte both shared a glance with her, and the three of them threatened to giggle. Lizzy managed to choke down the urge by sipping her tea, and Charlotte let out a snort that she turned into a cough. She suspected Anne was being deliberately mischievous by bringing up such a subject, and Lizzy nodded her subtle approval.

"There seems to be a great deal going on underneath the surface between you and my cousin."

Lizzy frowned she looked at Mr. Darcy. "I beg your pardon. I have not behaved at all improperly with the colonel—"

He looked surprised for a moment, and then he smiled. "I was referring to Anne, Miss Bennet. You seem thick as thieves with her."

"Goodness knows, she could use some friends, and she is quite a lovely woman with a sharp sense of humor."

Fitzwilliam seemed surprised. "Is she? I fear, she has never shown that to me despite our many years of acquaintance."

"You love her like a brother though."

He nodded. "Of course, I love Miss Anne, but I do not particularly know her. Truthfully, I thought there was little to her beyond what is on the surface."

"You are sorely mistaken then, Mr. Darcy. Surely, as often as you are wrong, you would be used to that by now, of course."

His eyes narrowed. "To what do you refer specifically, Miss Bennet?"

"I assume you are the one who prompted the Bingley party to decamp from Netherfield shortly after the ball?"

He nodded, looking proud of himself. "It was obvious he would be led to ruin if he stayed there."

Lizzy gasped. "Surely, you do not expect my sister would have tried to compromise Mr. Bingley?"

He arched a brow. "Perhaps not Miss Bennet herself, but I would not put anything past your mother, Miss Elizabeth."

She stiffened slightly at the easement of restrictions and formalities between them when he adopted her first name, but she couldn't deny his words. "I would like to think my mother would never be that desperate, but I cannot completely claim she would never act in such a fashion. Still, you did Jane and Mr. Bingley a great disservice by parting them."

"I used my best judgment in the matter, for it was obvious Miss Bennet did not have true regard for Bingley."

What had started out as an attempt to needle him was certainly going downhill quickly. Her immediate instinct was to jump to Jane's defense, which would certainly shorten the duration of teatime. She made a conscious effort to hold back and was relieved when Anne spoke up minutes later, saying, "Perhaps we could take a walk before we are due back to Rosings Park. Mama disapproves of me getting exercise, and I miss it."

Lizzy winced on her friend's behalf, but neither gentleman present seemed to realize there was anything untoward about what she'd said, indicating she regularly exercised otherwise. Anne looked briefly alarmed as well, and color came to her cheeks.

"Are you unwell, Anne?" Lizzy asked as the Colonel put his hand on her shoulder. The gesture was technically too intimate, but neither Anne nor Richard seem to mind. Lizzy thought it was encouraging, and Fitzwilliam seemed completely oblivious to it all. Charlotte was grinning her approval as well, having been taken into Anne's confidence during one of their book society meetings.

"Quite well. I suppose I am just excited about a walk."

"Yes, a walk would be refreshing." Lizzy stood up, looking at the colonel. "Will you walk with us, sir?"

"I would walk to the ends of the Earth for you two," said the colonel with a dashing smile and a flourish of his arm as he extended it for Anne to accept. After a moment, he started to offer Lizzy his other arm.

At that moment, Darcy had done the same, and though Lizzy was loath to spend time with him, she also wanted to allow Richard and Anne some time alone, so she slid her arm through Fitzwilliam's and sent a look at Charlotte. "Will you join us, dear friend?"

Charlotte hesitated and then shook her head. "I am feeling a little off today, Lizzy, so I believe I will take a rest."

Lizzy assumed her friend was being tactful, so she nodded her agreement. "I shall return in a while."

In minutes, they were strolling across Rosings Park grounds. At first, Lizzy and Fitzwilliam walked in step with the couple beside them, but Lizzy wanted to give them some time to be alone, so she implemented Charlotte's technique for handing her the book the other day. "Ouch."

Darcy frowned as she paused. "What troubles you, Miss Elizabeth?"

"I think there might be something in my shoe." She hobbled over, fearing she was appearing melodramatic, and leaned against a tree so she could remove her shoe. Without a button hook, it was proving difficult, which worked in her favor, because it allowed more time and space to lapse between them and the couple now moving ahead.

She was surprised when Mr. Darcy knelt on the ground, seeming uncaring of the knees of his breeches, and unbuttoned the shoe for her. He handed it to her, and she made a show of tipping it out and ensuring there was nothing remaining. Of course, there had been nothing in there to start with, but she was committed to the act now.

She leaned forward to put on her shoe again and stumbled. Mr. Darcy's quick reflexes saved her, but it brought his face temptingly close to hers. One of the scenes of the romance novels she had read ran through her mind, and she couldn't help wondering what it would be like to have Darcy's mouth on hers.

She quickly stepped away, brought back to reality by the thought, and assured herself it was prompted from reading romantic flights of fancy, not because she had any regard for Mr. Darcy. "Thank you for your assistance. I am fine now."

"Then shall we continue walking?" He held out his arm.

Lizzy wanted to refuse, but she put her arm through his anyway. As they continued onward, she had the sinking sensation the reason she wanted to avoid holding his arm wasn't because she found him so appalling anymore. Rather, it was because he was starting to become appealing, which greatly alarmed her.

Chapter Four

SHE DIDN'T SEE ANNE or Mr. Darcy again until the following night, when they once more joined Lady Catherine at Rosings Park for dinner. For Lizzy, the meals frequently came with a side of indigestion from having to deal with the judgmental and condescending woman. Compounded by having Fitzwilliam present, she hadn't been able to eat much the last few times they had visited.

Tonight, she and Anne managed to find a few minutes to whisper together ostensibly over sheet music for Anne, who'd agreed to play the pianoforte for them. Lizzy had discovered she had quite a talent for it at a previous visit, though Lady Catherine had been unable to let Anne have even that moment. She'd hastily assured everyone that if she'd had time to learn, she would have been a master of the pianoforte as well, far exceeding her daughter's own meager talents.

Anne had seemed impervious to the insult, but Lizzy hadn't missed the way Richard had stiffened, as though poised to say something. That led her to ask Anne if there was any progress as they held sheet music and whispered.

"Our walk was refreshing, and we got to speak, but I do not think anything has changed on his side. Truthfully, the only thing to change on my side are my feelings have grown stronger."

"You must tell him that, Anne."

Her friend looked horrified. "I could never be so bold, Lizzy. I am not like you."

Lizzy frowned. "What do you mean?"

"I have no doubt you would bravely and boldly declare your interest in a man who seemed indecisive about his affections."

Lizzy was flattered by the assumption, but she was also nonplussed by the realization she most likely would not. "Perhaps I would not, but in your case, I feel strongly that you should. It seems your cousin has equal affection for you, but one of you must have the strength and courage to voice it."

Anne winced slightly, missing a note on the pianoforte. "I could never."

With a sigh, Lizzy moved away, not wanting to further distract her and open her to more criticisms from Lady Catherine about her lapses while playing.

She found herself drifting across the room, heading toward Charlotte, but soon intercepted by Mr. Darcy. She wasn't entirely surprised, and her heart fluttered in her chest in a strange way as he stopped beside her. "Why are you and Anne always conspiring about something?"

She frowned at him, feigning annoyance. "I do not want to know what is going on in your mind, Mr. Darcy, but you are being ridiculous. We are not conspiring. We were merely talking." With that set down, she walked across the room to join Charlotte. Unfortunately, that brought her in contact with Mr. Collins and Lady Catherine, but she endured until dinner was called. She was able to successfully dodge Mr. Darcy for the rest of the evening.

SHE WENT OUT WALKING the next morning, unsurprised to find the colonel waiting for her. It had become the routine, and Anne had joined them once or twice over the last few days. That was probably predicated on being able to slip out without her mother knowing though, since Lady Catherine would raise a fuss about Anne being out in the fresh air.

He offered his arm in a polite gesture, and she took it as was expected, but there was no spark between them. Lizzy didn't want there to be, and she certainly didn't want the colonel to be attracted to her when she was convinced he loved Anne and vice versa. As they walked, she said, "You must tell me, Richard, do you love Anne?"

He stumbled to a halt, turning to face her. His arm dropped away from hers. "Why would you ask such an impertinent question?" His eyes narrowed. "I hope I am not giving you the wrong impression, Miss Bennet, but I am not in the market for a wife—"

Lizzy broke into laughter. "Do not be alarmed, Colonel, for I am not trying to get you to marry me. Nor am I ensuring there are no obstacles between us. I am simply curious if you care about Miss Anne. I believe you two would make a sound match."

Slowly, they started walking again, though he did not offer his arm this time. "There would be problems. For one, I do not think the lady in question holds me in that kind of regard."

"There is but one way to find out, and that is to ask her."

He seemed to mull it over. "I confess, I have fought in several campaigns against the French, but the idea of asking Anne such a simple question makes my stomach quiver."

Lizzy smiled. "I would think that's a good sign then, Colonel Fitzwilliam. Obviously, you have strong feelings for her, and I believe they are reciprocated."

He stopped again, turning her to face him. "She said something to you about it?"

Lizzy hesitated, unable to answer him without betraying Anne's confidences, so she searched for a delicate answer. "Let us just say, when a woman wishes to be courted, she shall make it plainly known. You must still take the first step." She leaned closer, making sure she could whisper to him, though she didn't expect they had any sort of audience. "It is my fervent wish that you make your feelings known to Anne, and I believe you will be happy with the results, Colonel."

When she stepped back, he was grinning broadly. "In that case, I shall speak to her immediately about courting."

"I am most happy to hear about the courting, Colonel Fitzwilliam." She laughed as he started to walk away before returning, looking embarrassed.

"If you will excuse me, Miss Bennet, I shall take my leave." He grinned, sounding and looking ridiculously happy. "I have much to do before I can officially began wooing."

She nodded her agreement and waved at him as he walked away. Once she was certain he was out of sight, she headed toward Anne's secret hideaway, where she hid her romance novels. Lizzy was about to start the final one in the box, and it made her both happy and sad. She was looking forward to reading about a rake that no one thought could be reformed, but she was also sad that it would soon be the end of the books. She could reread them, but none of them would have the same element of surprise during read-through again. She simply must acquire more of them when she was in London.

Chapter Five

FITZWILLIAM WAS OUT walking in a strictly random pattern. He was most certainly not looking for Miss Bennet, who'd taken to spending an inordinate amount of time with his cousin. He was concerned about that, and when he came across them, strictly by accident of course, he was further concerned by how close they stood for a moment. When she leaned closer, it looked like she might kiss him.

Fitzwilliam's stomach tightened at the idea, and anger hit him. He surged forward a few steps before regaining control of himself, and he paused close enough to hear most of the conversation, but far enough away for them not to see him. When Richard announced his intention to start courting, Fitzwilliam's guts clenched as acid burned up his esophagus. The thought was devastating.

Though he and Miss Bennet often spent their time verbally sparring, he felt like he'd gotten to know her more over the last few weeks of visiting Rosings Park. He had seen a softer side of her. When she let down her guard with him, she could be charming and enthralling. To his great discomfort, he reluctantly loved her.

He'd tried to fight it, of course, for it was a dreadfully terrible match. With the burden of her mother, her low connections, and her lack of achievements and accomplishments, she was hardly worthy to be a Darcy bride. Still, no matter how many times he reminded himself of that, it seemed futile to fight it.

Now, realizing his cousin was about to embark on courting Miss Bennet despite her lack of a large dowry, irritation compressed his chest and made it difficult to breathe. Resentment raged through him, and when the couple separated a moment later, he was undecided whether to follow Richard to make it clear he was staking a claim on Miss Bennet, or if he should follow Lizzy herself and stake the claim.

The way she looked around, seeming to be acting furtively, led him to choose to follow her instead. To his surprise, she crossed the grounds at a rapid clip, soon arriving at an old cottage. It looked broken-down, so his eyes widened when she walked up to the door, looked around again, and pushed against the metal frame that was there. She had to push it hard to open the door wide enough to slip in, and then it closed behind her.

His lips pursed, and he realized then she was up to something nefarious. Perhaps courting had been a special code word his cousin and Lizzy used to hide their plans to have an assignation instead. The idea of his cousin ruining her without even offering marriage was infuriating, and not just because he could barely stand the idea of imagining some other man's hands upon *his* Lizzy.

In a huff, he stomped across the grass, barely missing the muddy divot where rain had collected from the downpour the evening before, and strode to the door. Fortunately, he did not have to move the metal, so he didn't reveal his presence yet. He slipped in through the door, following her inside.

He paused for a moment to let his eyes adjust, though there was a lit lantern. It didn't provide a great deal of illumination but was enough to see the interior of the cottage was better than he'd expected. It appeared newer or at least safer than its outside, and he wondered how often Lizzy had been using this space for her assignations. Was Richard the first, or was he simply the current in a long line of unsuitable men she'd taken to her bed?

The idea left him angry and ill at the same time. He could hardly contemplate the idea of someone else lying with Lizzy, touching her skin, and teaching her the ways of passion. If it was going to be anyone, it should be him, but he feared he'd waited too long. Perhaps she was already well lost on the path to ruination.

If she were, he doubted he could redeem her. If she could not be redeemed, perhaps he could offer her a better situation as his mistress, at least until his passion for her burned out.

It was a scandalous thought to consider taking a daughter of the peerage as a mistress, but while his brain rejected it, his body endorsed the idea with the tightening of his cock.

He strode across the room after watching from the shadows as she knelt on the floor and removed a piece of floorboard. That didn't seem quite in line with the plan of seduction he'd thought she was enacting, and when she pulled out a box a moment later, he was further forced to question his theory.

He'd been moving quietly, but his foot hit a loose floorboard, which made her jump and turn to look at him. She let out a startled gasp, causing her hand to immediately go to her chest as she panted.

He frowned, certain what she had was something she didn't want him to see. He strode forward, pulling the chest from her hand when she tried to stop him. He opened it, surprised to find a collection of novels. He frowned and then looked at her. "What are these?"

"They are books, Mr. Darcy. I would think one as well-educated as you would know that." Her annoyed and aloof tone didn't hide the discomfort in her eyes or flushing of her cheeks. She appeared guilty, which only made him more curious.

As he looked down, reaching into the box to take out one of the books, he said, "You should know that if my cousin chooses to court you, nothing will come from it. It will not be an honorable courtship, for he cannot marry you without you being an heiress. He is the second son of an Earl, and therefore, his pecuniary situation is delicate. If you wish to surrender your maidenhead, assuming you still have it, you should wait for marriage."

She glared up at him. "How dare you say such audacious things to me? For one thing, I have no interest in your cousin courting me, Mr. Darcy, and for another, I shan't be doing anything of the sort. For my part, I could not care if I ever get married, for what woman gives up her freedom unless she is truly blinded by love?" She snorted. "What limited freedom there is for any woman."

He would have answered, but he was too shocked by what he held. He set down the box of books on the bed so he could open the one in front of him. When Lizzy darted forward, trying to take it from him, he subdued her against him with one arm holding her as she struggled while he opened the book with his other hand. It flipped to the last third of the book, to a well-worn page, and he let out a gasp of outrage upon realizing he was reading about a woman mounting a man. "Miss Bennet, where did you get this filth?"

She jerked it from his hand and put it back in the chest, closing it and trying to bend down to put it back. He grabbed her arm, keeping her from doing so. The chest tumbled to the floor, spilling out its contents and revealing the lurid covers. She didn't look at him as she tried to pull away so she could pick them up. "Answer me, Miss Bennet."

"Do let me be, Mr. Darcy. I promised no harm would come to these, and they mean a great deal to her." Lizzy shut off then, clamping her lips and glaring up at him.

Reluctantly, he let go of her arm, and she sank to her knees. As she struggled to put the books back into the chest, Fitzwilliam grappled with the knowledge that her mouth was perilously close to his ever-tightening groin. At the thought of putting his hand in her hair and dragging her head toward him, he let out a startled gasp and took a step back.

It was enough to bring some return of common sense, and he started across the room to exit the cottage. As he did so, they both froze at the sound of metal dragging against wood, and he continued rushing toward the door. He slammed into it, but it didn't budge. He tried for a few minutes, but someone had ensured they were trapped.

He turned to face Lizzy. "Was this your doing? Are you conspiring perhaps with Mrs. Collins to compromise me so I am forced offer for your hand?"

Lizzy's mouth gaped open, and then she let out a harsh laugh. "Your opinion of yourself is quite inflated, Mr. Darcy, and I assure you unwarranted. Were I feeling so masochistic, I would likely run myself through with a set of kitchen knives. It would no doubt be less painful than being forced to marry you."

His lips compressed as he stomped back toward her, but she didn't even look up as she busied herself with returning the books to the hidden place and repositioning the floorboards. "You can hardly fault me for doubting your word or your morals after seeing your choice of reading material."

She rolled her eyes as she stood up. "You are overthinking it, Mr. Darcy. These are escapist fantasies and nothing more. Truthfully, they set quite unrealistic expectations of what a man would be like. I highly doubt he would be so loving, tender, and romantic. Men like you provide ample proof of that being a fiction." She snorted. "Also, if he were truly hung like a horse, that would undoubtedly be most uncomfortable." She flushed, seeming to realize her company. "Forget I said that."

"I shall not. I demand an accounting."

"I demand you mind your own business."

"We are at an impasse, Miss Bennet, for if I do not get a satisfactory explanation from you, I will be forced to tell Mr. Collins what I have discovered."

Lizzy paled, dropping down to the bed. It appeared to be at first glance a melodramatic action, but he realized she was genuinely trembling with dread, and he wanted to call back the threat. "Just tell me what I wish to know."

"You could ruin more than one life if you tell anyone about this, Mr. Darcy. I do not know why, but you men feel we must be shielded, which is utterly ridiculous. There is no harm in a little bit of romance."

"For goodness' sake, Miss Elizabeth, whatever you are reading is talking about a man being mounted by a woman."

She frowned at him. "You object to such an unnatural position?"

At the position question, he found himself stunned as he sat down beside her on the bed. "No, I do not suppose I object to that. It can be quite..." He trailed off, flushing as he realized to whom he was about to admit that. "Never mind."

She seemed intrigued. "No, do tell me, Mr. Darcy. It sounds as though you have experience with such things, so is it truly possible?"

He cleared his throat. "Perhaps not in such a flowery way as described by the brief passage I read, but the physical act is possible, yes."

She leaned forward slightly, eyes wide. "And are men truly comparable to stallions?"

Darcy let out an awkward laugh. "I do not have much experience in that area, save for my own, er, endowments, but I do not believe that to be the case. If so, surely married women would be forced to walk in a most awkward way."

Lizzy surprised him by grinning, obviously getting the gist of his off-color joke that he had no business making to a woman of quality. "Mr. Darcy, how delightfully surprising."

He groaned. "How crass of me to discuss such a thing in front of a lady. I do apologize, Miss Elizabeth."

"I was the one who asked. Truthfully, the books made me curious. Some of what I read seemed unlikely, and Mrs. Collins refused to confirm many of the details, at least regarding logistics if some things were truly possible."

Fitzwilliam's eyes widened. "You mean the vicar's wife has read this as well?"

It was obvious Miss Bennet hadn't intended to reveal that, and she groaned as she looked away. "You must forget I said that too, Mr. Darcy."

"Is that genuinely what you want, Miss Elizabeth? My silence?"

She nodded and hesitated. "Perhaps that is not all I want, but I am certain what I wish for would be terrible of me."

He licked his lips, his heart speeding up as the air around them seemed to change, crackling with a new kind of energy. She was slowly relaxing, and he was leaning much closer to her than propriety dictated. They shouldn't be sitting on the bed together, and they most certainly shouldn't be discussing the current topic of conversation. "What is it you want?"

She slanted him a glance, appearing to weigh it in her mind. "I have recently advised my friend that she should be bold and tell someone what she desires. I would be a hypocrite if I did not do the same." In spite of her strong words, she still seemed uncertain.

"Undoubtedly, and you do not strike me as the type of woman who would be too weak to ask for what she wants."

Lizzy licked her lips, and he couldn't help groaning as his gaze followed the path her tongue took around her plump contours. "Would you like a kiss, Lizzy?" He decided to make it easier and not force her to blatantly ask. Easier for both of them, though he feared he might not be able to stop with a single, chaste kiss.

Her eyes widened, and she seemed to be debating with herself. "I know you should be the very last man I would ever want to kiss me, Mr. Darcy, but you are here, and..." She licked her lips again. "I confess, I am most curious to see what it feels like. Are the authors correct in their descriptions?"

He tried to ignore his irritation at the way she'd phrased that, as though she only wanted to kiss him because he was convenient. He'd much rather use his lips for another purpose than exchanging barbs, so he strove to keep peace between them. "I like to consider myself a man of reason, and the only way to find out is to experiment." He spoke briskly, as though it was purely an academic matter, which belied the way his heart was racing in his ears, and how his shaft was pressing painfully against the fall of his pants.

She nodded her agreement, but before she could speak again, though her lips opened to do so, he put his mouth to hers.

She breathed contentedly against him as she sank into his arms, and he wrapped his arms around her. Her mouth was soft under his, her lips opening to allow free access, and he darted his tongue inside. She didn't seem shocked by the action. Surely, a tongue kiss would be nothing compared to what must be written in those books when he remembered the scene he'd read.

He was determined to live up to whatever romantic foolishness the authors had used to describe kissing. He buried a hand in her hair, uncaring about the hairpin he dislodged in the process, and tilted back her head. That allowed him even better access to her mouth, and his tongue dipped deeper, stroking the back of her tongue and swiping across her interior cheeks before she shyly pushed back against his.

He sucked on the appendage as she strained to get closer. Before he could think better of it, Darcy put a hand in her bodice, cupping her breast after working his way under the chemise. She moaned softly as he tweaked her nipple, tugging it to a hard point, before moving on to give the other breast similar treatment.

Lizzy cried out, arching her back and breaking the kiss. Apparently, she was in the throes of passion, and she might've expected something to catch her, but all she did was fall to the bed. She looked alarmed for a moment, but then Darcy bent forward to kiss her again, and any trace of fear disappeared.

He alternated between kissing her gently and more forcefully, and when she nipped him on the lip in her fervent passion, bringing pain with it, he gasped and pulled back slightly.

She looked alarmed. "Did I hurt you, Mr. Darcy?"

The moment struck him as absurdly funny, and he started to laugh. "I believe you might be able to call me Fitzwilliam under the circumstances, Lizzy."

She seemed to think that was even more shocking than the kiss they had shared, or that his hand was fondling her nipple, but then she must have realized the absurdity as well. After a moment, she burst into giggles. "I suppose you are right, Fitzwilliam. At least for the moment."

"Is a kiss all you desire?"

She bit her lip, looking shy and uncertain. "There are other things in the books."

"Like?" As he asked, he tugged on her bodice and untied her chemise, freeing her breasts. He started to lick one of her nipples, and she cried out as her hand burrowed into his hair, holding him against her.

"That," she said with a gasp as she arched her back, her hips canting in her fitful writhing, obviously in need of something.

Fitzwilliam knew exactly what her body craved, though he dared not offer her the full experience. He was as yet uncertain of her emotions and her motives, and he couldn't discount the idea this was all an experiment for her. The impetuous young lady could also be caught up in passion and giving him more than she'd planned to cede. He well knew how such emotions could cloud judgment.

He didn't want to be in the position where he was forced to marry her. It wasn't because he objected to the idea, for he had resigned himself to reluctantly loving her and eventually making an offer for her hand. Rather, he was certain she would be miserable to be forced into that, and they didn't need another challenge between them.

He lifted his head. "Perhaps you would prefer me touching you somewhere else?"

"My...quim?" She blushed fiercely as she asked that, closing her eyes and turning her head. Obviously, she was ashamed at uttering or perhaps even knowing the word.

Under other circumstances, Fitzwilliam might've been appalled as well, but at the moment, he was too caught up in desire. He smoothed her dress up to her knees, waiting to make sure she didn't protest. She still wasn't looking at him, but she didn't seem as tense as he brought the dress to her waist before pushing up her petticoats as well.

When he traced his hand up her thigh, she shivered and moaned, but she didn't pull away. In fact, she parted her thighs to allow his hand better access, and he soon sought out the slit in her petticoat.

That led to her wet heat, and she was soaking for him. Fitzwilliam wanted to taste her, but he contented himself with dipping his thumb inside her folds, feeling her grasping silk around him as he dragged his thumb up through her anatomy to find the sweet little bud he was certain would drive her crazy.

He started to caress it, lightly at first, as she tossed on the bed, arching her hips and whimpering as he pressed on the sensitive bundle of nerves. When he increased his pace and his intensity, she quickly matched him, indicating it was the right level. He didn't want to hurt her or overwhelm her. He simply wanted to see Lizzy fall apart in his arms and be the one to hold her while she came back together again.

With that goal in mind, he kept his gaze on her face as she slowly turned back to look at him. "Open your eyes, Lizzy. Recognize who is giving you this pleasure." His voice was choked and hoarse, not at all like him normally.

Slowly, her lashes drifted upward, and she looked at him. There was passionate intensity in her gaze, along with a tinge of wonder, and perhaps a little embarrassment. He was determined to see that completely eradicated, so he redoubled his efforts to please her. He slid his index finger an inch or two into her opening, pulling it in and out while he continued to rub her sweet pearl, which was glistening with her moisture.

She arched her hips frantically, clinging to the blanket on the bed as he pleasured her. He knew she was coming when her sheath started to contract around his finger, and more moisture than ever flooded his hand. She let out a low, keening cry that he bent forward to capture with his mouth to prevent unwanted scrutiny or discovery under the circumstances.

When she collapsed against the bed in a boneless heap, he stopped stroking her. After a long moment, he reluctantly withdrew from her cunny. How he'd love to sink his cock inside her, but that came with certain commitments he wasn't certain she would accept, and he refused to ruin her any more than he already had.

He stood up reluctantly, and they both froze at the sound of metal screeching against wood. He rushed to the door, hoping to see who had locked them in, but by the time he reached it, there was no one in sight. He stifled a curse and turned back to Lizzy, who was trying to right her appearance. Her hair was still a mess, and he moved forward, lifting a hand to put the hairpin back in place for her. It wasn't as perfect as her maid would have done, but it would do to get her back to Hunsford.

In the process, the scent of her arousal on his hand wafted to him, and his cock jerked in his breeches. How he longed to fully introduce her to all the delights he was now certain she'd never experienced. It was on the tip of his tongue to offer for her hand, but he held back. He didn't want her to think it was strictly because they were in a compromising position.

After a second, she cleared her throat and took a step back. She was clearly trying to sound normal and composed. "I must insist upon your discretion."

Fitzwilliam frowned. "I am highly unlikely to tell anyone that I had you sprawled on the bed with my hand in your cunny."

She gasped and flushed, pressing a hand to her chest. "Goodness, Mr. Darcy, that was not what I meant." Her repressive tone was enough to make his lips twitch. "I refer to the books. They are not mine, and they could cause trouble for the owner. If certain parties were to find out about her collection, that would negatively affect her. Do I have your word?"

He could've negotiated, perhaps trading silence for further liberties, but he didn't want to be a heel. In the scheme of things, particularly compared to what he'd done to her, having a stash of bawdy books was mild.

He suspected they must belong to the vicar's wife, and he wouldn't like to see Mrs. Collins subjected to hours, days, or perhaps even months of prolonged lecturing from her husband, who would no doubt tell Lady Catherine as well. No, he couldn't wish that fate on anyone. "You have my word, Miss Bennet." He said it with a hint of teasing as he took her hand and made the solemn promise. "May I escort you back to Hunsford?"

She frowned. "I do not believe we should be seen together. We have already risked damaging our reputations. If we were discovered..." She paled. "I feel you would be forced into a maneuver that would make you most unhappy, Mr. Darcy, and I would never wish to compromise you or for you to ask for my hand."

"I do not think it would be the most dreadful thing ever, Miss Bennet. Would it truly be so terrible? Obviously, we could have great passion between us."

She surprised him by nodding her agreement. "Precisely right. I suspect that might be why we argue so forcefully with each other, Mr. Darcy, but I have no wish to marry, and you will certainly want someone better than me. I do not even sketch or know any of the modern languages. I suggest we consider this afternoon an operation brought on by madness and never speak of it again."

Before he could agree or disagree—having every intention of refusing the idea entirely—she sped away from him. He thought about calling her back or chasing after her, but after a moment, he let her go.

He was nowhere done chasing Lizzy, but she was not yet ready to be caught, and this required discretion rather than charging in and trying to take over the situation. If he was instrumental in forcing her into a marriage she claimed not to want, he was certain he would put up a stumbling block between them that might never be surmountable.

Chapter Six

AFTER RESTORING SOME sense of calm and dignity to herself upon returning to Hunsford, Lizzy remembered Anne was due for tea, so she prepared for that. Charlotte wasn't joining them again, once more not feeling well.

Lizzy stopped to check on her, entering the Collins' room reluctantly. She didn't want to contemplate the things that happened in this chamber, especially after having gotten a glimpse of the possibilities herself that afternoon.

Charlotte was resting on a chaise lounge with her hands on her stomach. Lizzy approached. "Are you all right, dear friend?"

Charlotte had worn a dreamy expression, and now she smiled as she looked up at Lizzy. "I am quite well." She bit her lip for a moment as though contemplating something. "I must take you into my confidence, Lizzy, for I do not think I can go another moment without telling someone besides Mr. Collins."

Lizzy had an inkling of what to expect, so she wasn't entirely surprised when Charlotte revealed she was a few weeks pregnant. Lizzy leaned forward and hugged her. "Congratulations, Lottie. You must be thrilled."

Charlotte nodded in agreement. "Marriage is somewhat agreeable, but I think motherhood will be far more delightful."

"I am persuaded of that. You shall be a fine mother." After ensuring Charlotte was fine, other than being tired and requiring an afternoon nap, she left her friend's room and entered the parlor. There was a knock at the door moments later, and Mrs. Tesch showed in Anne. After serving the two of them tea, she left to return to the kitchen.

Anne sipped for a few minutes before she asked, "Did you enjoy your surprise?"

Lizzy's eyes widened. "What surprise?" Her thoughts immediately jumped guiltily to what she had done with Mr. Darcy that very afternoon.

"I saw Fitzwilliam follow you into the cottage, so I decided to give you some time alone." Anne grinned. "It is very clear to me that you and Fitzwilliam are in love. So, did you take advantage of the opportunity to have a nice *chat*?" She winked and put special emphasis on the word chat.

Lizzy flushed. "That was you? Oh, Anne, how could you? We could have been ruined. I might have been compromised, and he would have been forced to ask for my hand."

Anne frowned. "Is that not what you want? There so many sparks between the two of you, and you look at each other with unconcealed longing. It is much the way I look at Richard, and that is what gave me the courage to do such a thing. I assumed you would enjoy some time with him."

Lizzy shook her head. "We are not in love." Even as she voiced it, she wasn't certain, at least for her part. There was much she disliked about Mr. Darcy, but she couldn't deny there was an equal amount of attraction, and more tender feelings had come out for him during their acquaintance even before he'd shown her such passionate attention.

Perhaps she was allowing that afternoon's activities to shadow her perceptions, but she couldn't pretend there wasn't some accuracy to her friend's words when Anne spoke again. "I suggest you so vehemently reject the idea because you understand on a fundamental level how right I am. Perhaps you do not wish to love my cousin, but you so clearly do, Lizzy." Anne nodded firmly as she delivered that pronouncement.

Lizzy didn't want to further explore the idea, and she was eager to change the subject of conversation, lest she end up confessing to

Anne exactly how far she'd strayed off the path of propriety that very afternoon. She cleared her throat and asked, "Did Richard come to visit you yet? I was walking with him earlier, and something he said indicated he might be..."

Anne lit up, and it completely changed her seemingly plain demeanor. There was nothing like love to light up a woman, Lizzy thought rather fancifully, recalling it from one of the books she had read with her friends. In Anne's case, it was particularly true. "Is he calling on you?"

"He has announced his intentions to court me, though I think he is bursting with eagerness to propose. Of course, he must first speak with my mother, and I know she shall initially resist, but when she accepts that I do not wish to marry Fitzwilliam, and he is already spoken for anyway," She slanted a glance at Lizzy and winked at her, "I do not doubt she will be forced to accept the match. After all, Colonel Richard Fitzwilliam is a perfectly proper man for me to marry, and the Matlocks are unlikely to resist either, since I have a large dowry. There will probably be a few hiccups, and I do not expect my mother to immediately fall in line, but I am optimistic about the future. No doubt, you will soon be announcing your own courtship?"

Lizzy's mouth tightened. "You are imagining things—"

"Miss Bennet, Mr. Darcy is here to call upon you," said Mrs. Tesch as she entered the salon.

Lizzy stifled a sigh, not missing Anne's large grin of delight as she said, "I suppose you should show him in then."

When Darcy entered the room, Anne was giggling as she stood up. She nodded to him, which made her giggle harder, and she looked at Lizzy. "I await your good news as well, my friend." She nodded to her cousin once more. "Good day, Fitzwilliam. I shall see you at dinner." She was still chuckling to herself when she left.

Mr. Darcy looked bewildered. "What was all that about?" His eyes narrowed. "Does she know...?"

She hastily shook her head. "Of course not, Mr. Darcy. I am not eager to be leg-shackled to anyone and have no plans to divulge our indiscretion—even to Jane."

His lips twitched lightly. "At least I have been elevated to the generic vicinity of wanting to avoid *anyone* rather than just me specifically when it comes to being your husband. Perhaps you realize there are certain compensations that I might offer when we are wed?"

She flushed as she looked around, not wishing to have that conversation in the vicar's house. "Mr. Darcy, this conversation is bordering on inappropriate." Her eyes widened. "You speak very confidently of us being wed."

He nodded. "I had thought to give you space to reach the same conclusions, but my honor will not allow me to undertake the actions we did without making it right. At first, I thought I could allow what happened this afternoon to stand, but there must be consequences for both of us. We acted rashly, and I allowed myself to compromise you. I apologize staunchly for that, and the only way to address the wrong is with marriage. I have decided to approach your father for permission to marry you."

Lizzy's eyes widened, and she sniffed at him. "I do not wish to marry anyone, as I have made plain. There will be no consequences, for things did not progress far enough to make a child. Did they, Mr. Darcy? Unless my romance books are wrong, there were quite a few steps we did not undertake, so you may rest assured there is no reason for us to marry."

"I must be truthful, for to be otherwise would be hypocritical, do you not agree?"

She tightened her lips, hating that the man was turning her words back on her. She nodded anyway.

"Frankly, I have been considering my feelings for a while before this afternoon. I would like to think I would not have allowed matters to get so out of hand if I had not already decided to marry you. I do love you, Lizzy Bennet. It has been reluctantly embraced after a hard-fought battle. I struggled against it at every turn, knowing the burden I bring upon myself by taking on your family along with you, but I find you quite worth it."

Lizzy's mouth dropped open in shock, and she wondered if he could hear the insulting words coming from him. "I must say no, thank you." She kept the words tight and rigidly polite.

He scowled. "That is all I am to hear from you? Simply no, thank you?" He shook his head. "Do you not believe you owe me an explanation for your refusal after everything?"

"Very well. Here is an explanation for you. For one thing, you have wronged Mr. Wickham by cheating him out of his inheritance promised by your father."

He opened his mouth, looking angry and about to protest.

She left him no quarter to speak. "For another, I suspect you have done your best to keep Jane and Mr. Bingley apart. Am I wrong?"

After a delay, he shook his head. "You are not. I do not see that she loves my friend, and he deserves a true love match, not one brought about because of mercenary reasons. Miss Bennet's supposed love for him is thin, and I have no doubt it would evaporate if his fortune disappeared tomorrow."

"That is sufficient answer there. You would allow your thoughts and opinions to hold more weight than my sister's heart. You would allow her to be grievously injured, and indeed, your dear friend as well, by keeping them apart because of your opinion. As we all know, once your good opinion has been lost, it is never recoverable, and that is an obstacle I could never overcome. A man who would stand between my sister and her happiness is not a man I could love." Her voice broke on the last word.

He seemed frustrated. "You do not have to love me to wed me, Miss Bennet. I could easily force the situation by confessing what has happened."

She stomped her foot before marching toward him, angling an angry finger in his face. "Do not even consider the idea, Mr. Darcy. If you were to force me into such an untenable position, I swear to you I would make your life a living hell. I will not abide."

After a moment, he took a step back, though he was still clearly angry. "You are a foolish woman to turn down what I offer. Surely, I am in much higher esteem than any man you ever thought to catch."

"I never particularly wanted to catch any man, Mr. Darcy, and I ask you to leave this instant." Her finger was still angrily in his face.

He seemed like he might lunge forward then, taking her into his arms. If it hadn't been for the door opening, along with Mr. Collins calling a cheerful greeting, he might've done so.

Lizzy was afraid all her resolve and anger would have melted under the force of passion if he'd kissed her, so she was relieved for her cousin's timing. She quickly took a step back, not wanting him to know they had been arguing.

Darcy must have reached the same conclusion, because his expression cleared, and he nodded to her. His tone was cool and lacking inflection. "Goodbye, Miss Bennet."

"Goodbye, Mr. Darcy." She hoped she could say that truthfully, and that they would not encounter each other again while she was at Rosings Park. For any further dinners Lady Catherine issued an invitation to, she would simply have a headache. She might be deemed rude, but that was better than facing Mr. Darcy again.

Chapter Seven

FITZWILLIAM WAS IN his room, instructing his valet to pack up his things, when Richard entered the room. He nodded to his cousin. "I am about to depart this wretched place."

Richard seemed shocked. "We have not even been here a sennight yet."

"It has been at least a fortnight," countered Darcy. "Truthfully, it feels like it has been an entire twelve-month."

Richard smiled slightly. "I suspect this has to do with a certain brunette with whom you are constantly trading barbs?"

Fitzwilliam shrugged. "You might be correct in that estimation. I find it unbearable to stay near her for a moment longer."

"I am afraid I cannot come with you, old chap, for I have committed to staying here and courting Anne. Truthfully, I intend to wed her as quickly as I can convince Lady Catherine."

Fitzwilliam froze, and even his valet twitched. "What?"

Richard looked briefly uncomfortable. "In fact, I have had strong feelings for Anne for years, but I was afraid to admit to them. I did not think she had any particular regard for me. I was wrong."

Fitzwilliam shook his head, marveling at the change. "I did not expect that. I wonder if that is perhaps what she and Miss Bennet were constantly conspiring about. Cunning and manipulation is rampant in the Bennet women. After all, it is Miss Bennet's sister, Jane Bennet, who is trying to lure Charles into her trap."

Richard frowned. "Miss Bennet's sister is the woman you told me about who tried to acquire Bingley, from whom you had to steer him away?"

Fitzwilliam grunted at the valet, who had finally moved on to the next bag. "Do try to hurry, Watkins. I would like to leave before sundown."

Richard seemed doubly shocked. "You plan to leave tonight? Surely, your grand departure can wait until morning when it is safer to travel?"

Fitzwilliam started to reject that idea, but then he hesitated and shrugged a shoulder. "I suppose you speak sense."

"Since you seem receptive to advice, allow me to give you more. I do not know this Miss Jane, and I only know Mr. Bingley in passing, but I suggest conceivably you have misinterpreted the situation. Perhaps it would benefit you to reevaluate."

Fitzwilliam scowled. "She clearly does not hold him in high regard. Her responses to his proximity are tepid, and there is very little enthusiasm when she sees him."

Slowly, his cousin smiled. "Until I told you about it just now, would you have ever guessed Anne has deep and strong feelings for me, Fitzwilliam?"

He hesitated before slowly shaking his head. "Of course not."

"Because she is a shy lady, and she has fine breeding. Have you not noticed that women of our social status are encouraged to behave demurely and hide all true emotions? Is it possible you have misjudged Miss Jane Bennet, expecting a strong and forceful display of emotion when she has been trained all her life to behave moderately? Perhaps Mr. Bingley and Miss Elizabeth know Miss Jane Bennet better than you do."

He wanted to reject his words, but Fitzwilliam found himself in the uncomfortable position of being unable to mount a reasonable argument to do so. His cousin had a point, especially when reinforced with a reminder that Anne had shielded her emotions from Richard all these years as well.

Fitzwilliam had certainly never picked up on them. He wasn't close enough to Anne to be considered a confidant, and he doubted she would have ever mentioned such a topic or spoken of it with him under any circumstance. Still, she'd given no indication of her true feelings when she interacted with Richard.

A brief mental review of the times he could recall them relating left him still stymied to think she might truly love Richard. Yet he had no reason to doubt it, for Anne was not a grasping social climber in a desperate situation or dogged by a woman like Fanny Bennet to make a good match at all costs.

If a woman like her, with no reason to feign interest in a man, could hide her true emotions so effectively, was it not conceivable Miss Jane had done the same? He shook his head in surprise as the realization dawned on him. "I fear you have given me much to consider, Richard."

"I hope it will be what you need to hear to think clearly, Fitzwilliam, and to keep you from hastily fleeing away from a happy match for yourself as well. It strikes me that Miss Bennet would be eminently suitable for you."

Fitzwilliam scoffed. "Her family is lowbrow, and her connections are common. Her mother is a trial by herself, and only a foolish man would saddle himself with the Bennet family."

"A fool, or perhaps a man in love." Richard tossed that out as he moved to the door. "I do hope I still find you in attendance in the morning, Fitzwilliam."

"It is entirely possible, Richard," he said as his cousin disappeared. After a moment, he looked at Watkins, who was slowly packing, having dragged out the task. He wasn't the type to gossip, so Fitzwilliam suspected his valet had performed so slowly not to hear as much of the exchange as possible but because Watkins was expecting the very pronouncement he made a moment later when he said, "We might stay a bit longer, Watkins. Perhaps you have saved yourself some trouble with having to unpack everything again by your slowness."

The older man flushed slightly, but he inclined his head. "Very good, sir."

Fitzwilliam departed the room, finding he thought better when he was active. He ended up taking to the grounds of Rosings Park, walking through the rose gardens for hours. He didn't even bother to return to the house for dinner, and before he knew it, the moon was high in the sky.

By the time he'd settled matters in his own head, he was impatient to speak with Lizzy again. He could no longer hold back the impulse and rushed to Hunsford to have an audience with her.

To his disappointment, the house was dark, but he didn't let that stop him. He'd been in the rectory a few times, and he had a general orientation of where the general quarters were versus the bedrooms.

He moved down the side of the house, peeking into a curtain that was askew and soon identifying the master bedroom. That wasn't the room he wanted, so he moved farther down the house, unable to see in the next window.

He pressed his ear against it for a long time, unable to hear anything inside. Finally, deciding to be bold, and perhaps incredibly foolish, he tried the window. Unfortunately, it was sturdily locked. Short of breaking it, he wasn't going to get in through there.

At first, he thought he might have to wait until morning after all to approach Lizzy in the proper way, though his impatient frame of mind left him in no mood to do so. Only as he started to walk back to Rosings Park did he remember having seen Mr. Collins place a key on the door lintel one afternoon when they were all returning after having been at Rosings Park for tea. He'd been along upon having encountered them during a walk and accepted their invitation to dinner. Of course, it had been to be near Lizzy, but he'd denied that even to himself.

Feeling more optimistic, he turned back to the house and approached the front step. Soon enough, his fingers found the key on the lintel, and he used it to quietly unlock the door before returning the key, opening it, and sliding inside. He closed it softly, holding his breath the whole time, and then he crept through the rectory.

Part of him realized how foolish and reckless this was, but he was so focused on getting to Lizzy and explaining everything, along with telling her he'd had a change of heart, that he couldn't care. Reputation be damned.

He crept past the Collins' bedroom as quietly as possible, relieved to find the door closed. He heard snoring coming from within, and surely from the volume, it must be Mr. Collins. He could scarcely imagine Mrs. Collins being able to summon such a sound even if she tried.

Once he was past their room, it was a matter of two more doors from which to choose. One was the W.C., and he quietly closed it back, so the other had to be Lizzy's room. With a deep breath, he grasped the door, turned the handle, and slipped inside. He shut it quietly behind him, and as he started to turn, he saw something heading toward his face at an alarming rate.

It was instinct that had him lifting his hand and blocking the fire poker. Lizzy let out a small shout as he wrenched it from her and tossed it aside. He quickly clamped his hand over her mouth to keep her from crying out again, not wishing for Mr. Collins to discover his presence there, at least not until they'd settled a few things.

Her eyes went wide, but she relaxed in his arms, apparently recognizing him, so he slowly dropped his hand to let her take a step back. "Are you all right, Miss Bennet?"

She glared at him. "Other than having the fright of my life. I thought you were a robber, Mr. Darcy. What in the world are you doing in my room?"

"I am quite well too, thank you for asking. Fortunately, you managed not to hit my skull with that chunk of iron." He chuckled at her angry look. "I had to see you, Lizzy."

He was amused by the way her gaze immediately darted to the bed before looking back at him, and she seemed uncertain. "I do not think this is wise, Mr. Darcy. We have said everything there is to say."

"I have not come here to seduce you." His pants tightened at the thought, and he cleared his throat. "I have come to apologize. My cousin gave me much to think about this afternoon, and I realized I have unfairly judged your sister. I deemed her cold and uninterested when perhaps she is simply shy and accustomed to shielding her emotions."

To his surprise, Lizzy's mouth gaped open. She appeared truly shocked at his theory, making him second-guess himself.

A second later, she nodded. "That is exactly it, but how did *you* come to that realization?"

He was starting to feel insulted. He clamped his lips shut for a moment before he took a deep breath to rein in his anger. "I am capable of revised thought and forming second opinions, Miss Bennet."

"Not according to Miss Bingley."

"Perhaps Miss Bingley does not know me as well as she thinks." With that tart response, he moved closer. "With my new epiphany, I intend to withdraw all objections, and I shall suggest to Bingley that we return to Netherfield for the rest of his tenancy. Perhaps I shall do it under the guise of fishing and hunting to discourage Mrs. Hurst and Miss Bingley from accompanying us. I have no doubt I will be able to easily convince him to return. Once he is back near Miss Bennet, they will no doubt soon succumb to the feelings between them again."

She hesitated for a moment, looking like he was almost too good to be true. "You no longer intend to meddle?"

He chuckled. "Perhaps I will even play matchmaker. I suppose it could be viewed that way, since it will be my idea to return to Netherfield. Yes, you can consider me a matchmaker, though truthfully, I am doing it for you as much as for your sister and Bingley."

"I see." She looked confused but possibly hopeful.

He recalled her other objection from the afternoon. "As to George Wickham…" He paused at the way she stiffened, her lovely jaw clenching. He hoped she would believe him.

"The man is a scoundrel and a wastrel. He got his living in one lump sum after refusing to be the parson of Kympton and then tried to seduce my fifteen-year-old sister into eloping once I denied him any further funds."

Her eyes widened, and she seemed disbelieving. "He is a gentleman—"

"No. He has the education and was raised as one, but he is no true gentleman. He is a cad, Lizzy, and to think he might be the reason you deny me is unbearable."

She licked her lips, seeming to consider his words for a time. "Please tell me more."

With a sigh, since he really didn't want to discuss Wickham more than he had to, he spent the next several minutes pacing and recounting for her the true nature of Wickham. There were many instances of his poor behavior, but he kept it to the most shocking ones, including the poor housemaid he'd seduced at Oxford and left with child, turning her away without a second thought.

She was clearly shocked when he'd finished. "Your poor sister." She put a hand to her mouth. "And what of the maid he compromised while you were at Oxford?"

"She recovered from the illegal procedure, and I gave money to her and her sister to start over in Ireland. The last I heard in a letter of thanks from her sister was she had recovered and was being wooed by a law clerk."

Lizzy looked stunned. "I have certainly misjudged him. And I fear you as well, Fitzwilliam."

That she used his first name gave him a spark of hope. "Allow me to fervently state I wish to win you over, Lizzy, and I hope you will give me another chance now that you have a better accounting of my character."

Chapter Eight

LIZZY STARED AT HIM for a long moment, her gaze probing into what she hoped was the very heart of him. She wanted to believe him, and she didn't think Fitzwilliam was the type of man who would say anything to get what he wanted. Indeed, he had been honest to a fault on many occasions. Bluntly honest. Perhaps even too honest. It seemed unlikely he would lie to her about his change of heart for Jane and Bingley or that scoundrel, Wickham. "What of my family? You so reluctantly love me, and you fight it because of them. I fear they shall never live up to your standards."

"I would take ten of your mother if it meant having you, Lizzy. I do love you, and it is no longer with reluctance but great enthusiasm. I fought against it, and I cannot pretend I didn't. I did not want to love you, but I do. With great sincerity and enthusiasm, I truly love you."

She couldn't hold out any longer. Lizzy stepped closer and melted into his arms. "Perhaps I should disbelieve you, but I find the idea of you being untruthful laughable, Fitzwilliam. I do believe you. I believe you fought long and hard against loving me, because I have done the same."

He let out a ragged breath. "You fought loving me?"

She nodded slowly.

He seemed to be in agony as he asked, "Pray, what was the outcome, Lizzy? Were you successful in fighting your feelings?"

It gave her great pleasure to slowly shake her head. "In fact, I was not, Fitzwilliam. I love you."

With a ragged exhalation, he hugged her tighter. "In that case, I am asking you to marry me. I doubt your father will have any objections."

Lizzy laughed. "I believe you might be wrong on that account, but not because he will object to you. Truthfully, my father will not want to part with me, but he will understand it must be done at some point in time. Though I imagine he has clung to the hope that I am sincere when saying I never wish to marry."

He looked troubled. "And is that true?"

Lizzy bit her lip and nodded slowly. "It was true, at least until I met you. I have had cause to revise my opinion of the state and my stance on it over the last few months, and I have concluded there is a time and place for marriage. When there is love, trust, and respect, it is acceptable to yield. I trust you to look after my best interests, Fitzwilliam."

"I promise I shall."

Lizzy turned to look at the bed then. "You do not envision a long engagement, do you, Fitzwilliam?"

He frowned. "No more than a month, I should think."

She shook her head. "I think that is far too long to wait."

He frowned. "Wait for what?"

"I have many questions, and there is much I want to experience based on the books I have read. Yes, you simply must confirm for me that what the authors have written is true, or allow me to disprove it as romantic nonsense."

His frown grew. "I am confused about what you want, Lizzy."

Feeling a little shy, she took his hand and led him to the bed. "Shall I make it clear, Mr. Darcy?"

With a chuckle, he pulled her into his arms and kissed her with exceeding thoroughness. "It is quite crystal-clear now, Miss Bennet."

As he lowered her to the bed, joining her on it, Lizzy strove to relax. The experience was a little nerve-racking, and she couldn't pretend she wasn't nervous, but she felt utterly confident in the man she'd chosen. When his mouth covered hers, she surrendered to his masterful kisses, finding them even more delightful than they had been earlier.

His hand skimmed her breasts, finding her nightgown was no impediment. Lizzy was soon naked, so she stood up when he did as well.

He frowned at her. "Is something wrong?"

She shook her head. "I assumed you might need assistance with undressing? Gentlemen have valets, do they not?"

He smiled. "Perhaps I could use some aid."

She moved closer, slowly working out the complicated knot of his cravat before unwinding the long fabric. By the time she'd removed the starched insert, he'd unbuttoned his shirt and removed it, along with unbuttoning the fall of his trousers and letting them fall to the floor. He stepped out of them, revealing his full glory to her, and her eyes widened.

"Not entirely like a horse, but far too close." She laughed, though she was a little frightened. "I do not see how that will be possible."

"I assure you it shall, Lizzy."

Feeling mischievous, she slowly sank to her knees. "I suppose I should verify for myself. Surely, if it will fit in my mouth, it will fit elsewhere?"

He groaned, closing his eyes as he put a hand in her hair. "I should say you do not have to, and of course, you do not, but I will be most appreciative if you do, sweet Lizzy." His eyes opened then. "How have you discovered such an act?"

"Why Anne's books, of course, Fitzwilliam."

He gasped. "Anne's? I thought for certain they must be Mrs. Co...oh..."

With a grin, she placed a kiss to the tip of his shaft before wrapping her mouth around him and cutting off his words. She was pleased by the way he jumped in her hand. The authors must have written with some knowledge of such things, so she relied on what she'd read as a guide of how to proceed.

"Less teeth," said Darcy with a slight hiss as she encompassed his shaft and slid it deeper into her mouth.

Remorseful, Lizzy immediately shielded his skin from her teeth as she teased and tasted him with her tongue until he was thrusting frantically against her face. She wasn't certain what would happen at culmination, though she'd read about it in the books Anne had shared with her. She didn't find out though, because Mr. Darcy pulled away as his shaft tightened.

He was shaking, and he seemed on the edge of release, so she didn't protest when he lifted her and put her on the bed. Her legs fell open, and she expected him to claim her. Instead, he laid down between them. Her eyes widened, but she wasn't shocked to realize he planned to kiss her quim. She'd read of it, so she held her breath with anticipation.

He parted her thighs wider as he worked his way inward from kissing her outer skin. She let out a soft moan of eagerness as his lips hovered against her lower area, and when his tongue slipped inside her, she was lost.

Lizzy reached for her night-rail on the bed, stuffing it in her mouth to keep from crying out as his lips and tongue proved to be equally exciting on her quim as they had been in her mouth. No, unquestionably more so.

He worked her to a fevered state, and she writhed and moaned, rolling against him as she arched against his hold, though he held her securely against the bed. Fortunately, it wasn't overly creaky, because she didn't want Charlotte and Mr. Collins to interrupt them. She was too far gone to stop what they were doing, and she feared the vicar and her best friend would have had quite a distressing scene play out before them if they had intruded right then.

When his tongue darted inside her before he gently sucked on her pearl, she came apart in his arms with a strong cry. The night-rail mostly muffled it, and as she started to come down, spitting out the cloth, he moved between her legs.

Fitzwilliam held her tenderly, and she realized he was flipping positions. Her eyes widened a moment later when she found herself sitting astride, his cock pressing against her opening. "Truly?"

He smiled. "I am told it is most enjoyable for a woman this way, and you seemed so curious about it."

She flushed, but she could hardly deny that. It was one of her favorite scenes from that book, and she'd already reread it a few times during her stay.

Having some experience simply from the written word, she knew to grasp his shaft at the base. She did her best to line it up, and he accommodated her by moving around, helping her position properly.

Slowly, she sat on him as he sank inside her, and though it hurt for a moment, making her pause and wince, she gritted her teeth and endured the suffering. If the books could be believed—and she had no reason to doubt them as of yet—it would soon get better.

As the pain started to fade, the sting turning into a pleasant ache that demanded more, she began to ride him. Fitzwilliam cupped her hips, holding her astride his lap as he thrust upward while she pushed down against him. She was consumed with need, and her gaze locked with his.

As their bodies fused, straining toward completion, she swore her heart was entwining with his as well. Their emotions were surely merging, and she could practically feel how much he loved her. Her love swelled to match, and she clung to his shoulders when she started to climax. She closed her eyes, forced to break the connection between them under the intensity of her emotions and pleasure, and she somehow managed to hold in a shriek of pleasure when she came.

Fitzwilliam groaned as well, but he muffled it by clamping his lips. His fingers dug deeply into her hips for a long moment as he held her against him. He filled her with waves of his release, and she crashed against him an instant later, sprawling across his chest as he pressed a kiss to her forehead.

"Tell me, Lizzy, did it live up to your romantic books?"

Slowly, she lifted her head and smiled knowingly. "You far exceeded them, Mr. Darcy. Authors should write about you, for you are truly the pinnacle of male achievement."

He flushed, looking more embarrassed than pleased, but he laughed. "How I love you, Lizzy."

"I love you too, Fitzwilliam. I cannot imagine all the different ways we might explore that love, but I know one thing."

He arched a brow. "What is that?"

"I am going to require at least a full bookshelf at Pemberley, and I shall likely need your connections to obtain the literature I require, since it is scandalous and possibly illegal. I have no doubt Anne shall come to visit us often, and perhaps even Lottie, so that we might trade books. After all, as much as I love you, I cannot have you interrupting my book society."

He laughed as he softened inside her, slowly pulling her away from their fused bodies to lie beside him as he turned onto his side as well. "I am happy to arrange such indulgences for you, madam. I endeavor only to make you happy as Mrs. Darcy."

She wrapped his chest hair gently around her finger. "I have no doubt you shall do that in every way, Mr. Darcy, and will certainly exceed every expectation."

Epilogue

IT WAS A BEAUTIFUL May day as three couples assembled at the church in Meryton because of its central location. There were a few guests in attendance, including Lady Catherine. She appeared reluctant to be there, but she must have consigned herself to the idea that her daughter was about to wed Colonel Richard Fitzwilliam, though he was a colonel no more. He had resigned his commission and would soon step into the role of assisting Lady Catherine with running Rosings Park.

Anne looked positively radiant in her light-pink gown, and her new bonnet framed her face, highlighting the vibrant color that remained constantly in her cheeks. She had blossomed in the intervening weeks since Richard's proposal, and Lizzy was not surprised that Anne's soon-to-be husband couldn't take his eyes from her.

Her gaze moved to the next bride, her dear sister, Jane, who looked stunning in a light-yellow gown and ivory bonnet. She stood with Mr. Bingley, who seemed as besotted as Colonel Fitzwilliam while he held onto Jane's arm. She smiled her approval at the devotion between them before turning to look at her own groom.

Mr. Darcy stood beside her, his arm through hers, and he was dashing in his wedding finery. She had chosen a pale blue frock and a matching hat with an ivory ostrich feather. It was an outrageous expense, but her mother had insisted, and she'd happily obliged. It was what she'd liked after all, and she didn't want anything about the day to be imperfect.

She was certainly getting the perfect groom, at least for her. She and Fitzwilliam would probably always quarrel, but truthfully, there was a fun element to their arguing that she suspected was a form of foreplay. She had not realized that until reading Anne's books and gaining some experience of her own, but now she could easily tell what had simmered between them almost from the start was sexual tension more than dislike.

As the vicar started the ceremony, she turned to stand beside him instead of facing him and happily gave her promise to be his devoted wife. Though she had long been resistant to the idea of marrying, with it taking Mr. Darcy to change her mind, she was happy she had been able to reconsider her opinion and find a new conclusion, just as he had regarding her sister.

When they were wed, Fitzwilliam pressed a gentle kiss to her lips. She wanted to deepen it, but that would be scandalous, and she knew they had tonight. There had not been a chance to repeat their night of intimacy, and she'd been impatiently waiting during the past six weeks.

That would come soon enough, and they would have years together to explore every variation of passion either of them could imagine. Thanks to a discreet gift from Fitzwilliam just a few days ago, she had an entirely new box of books to read and mine for inspiration once the business of getting married was behind them. She would likely start reading on her honeymoon, since it was three days to Pemberley from Longbourn.

She could hardly wait to start the reading or the passionate play with her husband, but surely, she could endure the wedding breakfast first before they slipped away to their shared room at Longbourn and consummated their marriage. They would be on the way to Pemberley soon enough, but tonight was all about them.

For now, she would give her mother this day, and she would even enjoy parts of it herself, but her thoughts were mostly on what would come later rather than what was happening right now. She could hardly wait for Fitzwilliam to hold her again. This time, she would be Mrs. Darcy, and the thought gave her a giddy thrill as her husband stole one more kiss after they exited the church before heading to the waiting coach-and-four.

A barouche waited for the rest of the bridal party, but Lizzy and Fitzwilliam headed to the smaller one built for two plus a driver. She wanted every possible moment alone with Fitzwilliam that she could have. If she arrived at Netherfield for the wedding breakfast looking a little disheveled, she doubted it would shock anyone.

If it did, she didn't care. She quickly decided that as Fitzwilliam kissed her once again, giving her a preview of what awaited them later in the afternoon and for the rest of their lives.

Want to know a secret? We do, too! What happens behind closed doors between Mr. Darcy and his Elizabeth? Find out in our shared series, Mr. Darcy's Secret Stories. Each steamy, heartfelt book can be read in one afternoon (or evening!) as each author imagines new ways for Mr. Darcy to show Lizzy his eternal devotion. And maybe how he looks in a dripping wet shirt. You know, both are good. Discover all of Our Dear Couples' secrets in this new series of Pride and Prejudice variations.

https://www.darcysecretstories.com

PLEASE SIGN UP FOR Abbey's newsletter[1] to receive information about new releases. If you have any difficulties, email Abbey to request a manual add.

---

1. https://www.subscribepage.com/JAFF

About The Author

ABBEY IS A DIEHARD Jane Austen fan and has loved Fitzwilliam since the first time she "met" him at age thirteen upon borrowing the book from the school library. He is the ideal man, though Abbey's husband is a close second. Abbey enjoys writing various steamy and sweet Jane Austen variations, but "Pride & Prejudice" (and Mr. Darcy) will always be her favorite

Did you love *Mischief & Matchmaking: A "Pride & Prejudice" Variation*? Then you should read *Mistaken Masquerade: A Pride & Prejudice Variation*[1] by Abbey North!

[2]

A midnight tryst, mistaken identities, and perhaps a passion that could last a lifetime?

Lydia has been a naughty girl and has George Wickham convinced Uncle Gardiner has given her a generous dowry. Lizzy is determined to protect her sister from the scoundrel, so when she intercepts a note suggesting a midnight tryst in the library at the Netherfield Masquerade Ball, she intends to warn him away permanently. Mr. Darcy intercepts the same note, believing Lizzy is the one having the tryst with Wickham, and he is determined to save her from herself. With mistaken

---

1. https://books2read.com/u/mBzd9O

2. https://books2read.com/u/mBzd9O

assumptions and confused identities, who is meeting in the library, and what consequences will it bring for ODC?

While Abbey sometimes writes sweet JAFF, this is strictly sensual.

Also by Abbey North

A Month To Love
Reproach (Part One)
Resentment (Part Two)
Rapport (Part Three)
A Month To Love Compilation

Crime & Courtship
Rapacity & Rancor: A Pride & Prejudice Variation
Abduction & Acrimony : A Pride & Prejudice Variation Mystery Romance
Extortion & Enmity: A Pride & Prejudice Variation Mystery Romance
Murder & Misjudgment: A Pride & Prejudice Variation Mystery Romance
Perfidy & Promises: A Pride & Prejudice Variation Mystery Romance
Crime & Courtship: A Sweet Pride & Prejudice Mystery Romance Compilation

Darcy's Courtesan
Adversity (Darcy's Courtesan, Part One)
Avidity (Darcy's Courtesan, Part Two)

Amity (Darcy's Courtesan, Part Three)
Darcy's Courtesan: A Sensual "Pride & Prejudice" Variation

Marriage & Mysteries
Honeymoon & Hemlock

Mr. Darcy's Secret Stories
Mistaken Masquerade: A Pride & Prejudice Variation
Mischief & Matchmaking: A "Pride & Prejudice" Variation

Standalone
Christmas At Pemberley: A Pride & Prejudice Variation
A Scandalous Proposition: A Pride & Prejudice Variation
Shadow of Darcy: A Sensual Pride & Prejudice Paranormal Variation
Darcy's Obsession
Blackmailing Lizzy: A "Pride & Prejudice" Variation
Darcy's Wicked Game
Danger With Darcy: A Sensual "Pride & Prejudice" Variation
Passion & Prostrations: A Sensual "Pride & Prejudice" Variation
Darcy's Debt: A Sensual Pride & Prejudice Variation
Obstinacy & Obligation: A Sweet Pride & Prejudice Variation
Heartsick: A Sweet "Pride & Prejudice" Variation
Darcy's Alibi: A Sweet "Pride & Prejudice" Variation
Marooned With Darcy: A Sensual "Pride & Prejudice" Variation
Compromising Mr. Darcy: A Steamy "Pride & Prejudice" Variation
Marrying Mr. Darcy: A Sensual "Pride & Prejudice" Variation
Darcys' First Christmastide

www.ingramcontent.com/pod-product-compliance
Lightning Source LLC
Chambersburg PA
CBHW021746150726
47989CB00004B/1537